To Allison
Merry Christmas
Love,
Aunt Marianne
and
Uncle Barry

Classic Fairy Tales

ADAPTED BY LUCY KINCAID
ILLUSTRATED BY ERIC KINCAID

CHEX BOOKS · NEW YORK

Cinderella

Cinderella lived in a big house.
She was always busy. Her two
stepsisters made her work hard.
"Cinderella! Sweep the floor!"
"Cinderella! Wash the dishes!"
"Make the beds!"
"Clean the windows!"
Cinderella's work was never done.

Her stepsisters spent half the day
telling Cinderella what to do.
They spent the other half trying
to make themselves pretty.
"Cinderella!
Brush my hair!"
"Cinderella!
Tie my bow!"

"Powder my nose!"
"Fasten my buttons!"

One day a letter arrived at the house.

"There is to be a ball at the palace. We are invited!" shouted the stepsisters.

"Am I invited?" asked Cinderella.

"Even if you are, you cannot go," said her step-sisters. "You will be too busy getting us ready."

The day of the ball came. The
stepsisters kept Cinderella very
busy indeed. There was so much
to do. Poor Cinderella did not
know what to do first.

At last, the stepsisters had gone
and the house was quiet. Cinderella
sat by the fire and began to cry.
"If only I could
go to the ball,"
she wept.

"You SHALL go to the ball," said a voice behind her. Cinderella jumped up in surprise. She thought she was alone in the house.

"Who . . . who are you?" she gasped.

"I am your Fairy Godmother," said the stranger.

"I have come to get you ready for the ball."

"Bring me a pumpkin,"
said the Fairy
Godmother. She
turned the pumpkin
into a coach.

"Bring me four
white mice," said
the Fairy Godmother.
She turned the
mice into four
white horses.

"Bring me three
lizards," said the
Fairy Godmother.
They became a
coach-driver and
two footmen.

"I cannot go to the ball dressed
in rags," said Cinderella sadly.

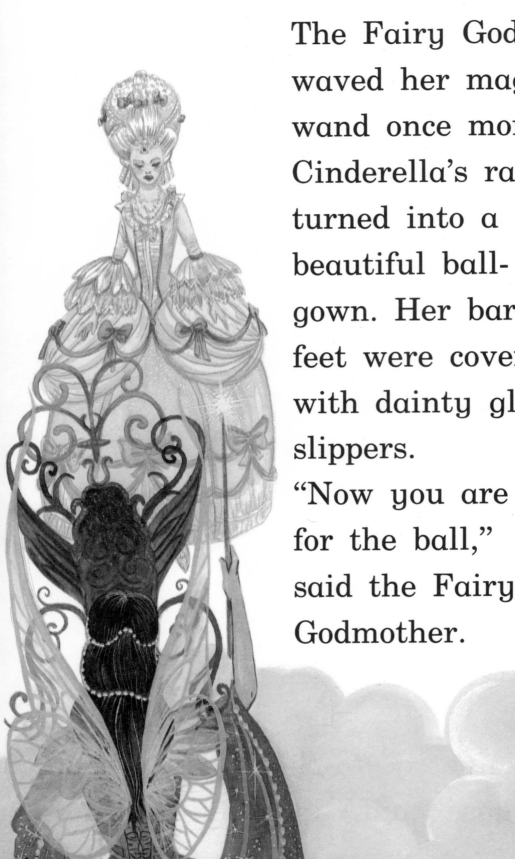

The Fairy Godmother waved her magic wand once more. Cinderella's rags turned into a beautiful ball-gown. Her bare feet were covered with dainty glass slippers.

"Now you are ready for the ball," said the Fairy Godmother.

"But first, a warning. You must
leave before the clock strikes
twelve. At twelve everything will
change back again."

"I will remember," said Cinderella.

"Thank you, dear Fairy Godmother."

Cinderella danced all night with the Prince. Her stepsisters saw her, but they did not know it was Cinderella. They thought she was a princess.

Cinderella was so happy she forgot all about the Fairy Godmother's warning. Then the palace clock began to strike the chimes of midnight. One . . . two . . . three . . . "I must go!" cried Cinderella and she ran from the palace.

"Stop! Stop!" cried the Prince.
Cinderella did not hear him. As
she ran down the palace steps she
lost one of her glass slippers.
. . . ten . . . eleven . . . TWELVE!!!

The beautiful gown turned into rags.
The coach turned into a pumpkin.
The mice and the lizards ran away.

The Prince found
her glass slipper
lying on the
palace steps.
He called to
a footman.

"Take this slipper
and find its
owner. I will
marry the girl
it fits."

The footman travelled all over the kingdom with the slipper. It fitted no one. At last he came to the house where Cinderella lived.
"Let me try it!" said one of the stepsisters. She snatched the slipper from the footman. "Look!" she cried. "A perfect fit."

"No it is not!" shouted the other stepsister. "Your heel is hanging out. Give it to me!" She snatched the glass slipper.

It didn't fit her either, though she tried to pretend that it did. "Is there anyone else in the house who should try the slipper?" asked the footman.

"No!" said both stepsisters together.

"Yes there is," said their father.

"Cinderella has not tried it yet."

"The Prince would never marry HER!"
laughed the stepsisters.
"The Prince said everyone must try
the slipper," said the footman.
It fitted Cinderella perfectly.

Her stepsisters were so surprised
they fainted.

The stepsisters still looked
surprised when the Prince and
Cinderella were married.

All these appear in the pages of the story. Can you find them?

Cinderella

stepsisters

letter

Fairy Godmother

coach

pumpkin

glass slipper

Prince

Use the pictures to tell the story
in your own words, and then draw
your own pictures.

Hansel and Gretel

Once there was a woodcutter. He was very poor. One day he said to his wife, "What will become of us? We are so poor we cannot feed the children."

His wife said, "We will take the children into the forest and leave them there. They must take care of themselves."

Hansel and Gretel
were listening at
the door. Gretel
began to cry.
"What will become
of us?" she said.
"Do not cry,"
said Hansel.
"I will look
after you."

When it was dark
Hansel went into
the garden. He
filled his pockets
with pebbles. Then
he went to bed.

Next day the woodcutter took the
children into the forest. His wife
gave them both a piece of bread.
Hansel's pockets were full
of pebbles. Gretel had to put
the bread in her apron.

Hansel kept looking back at the house. "What are you looking at?" asked the woodcutter. "I am looking at my little cat," said Hansel. But really he was dropping pebbles on the path.

When they were deep in the forest
the woodcutter made a fire.
"Sit and rest," he said to Hansel
and Gretel. "When we have cut the
wood we will come back for you."
Hansel and Gretel waited and waited.
Their father did not return.
At last they went to sleep.

When Hansel and
Gretel woke, it was
dark. They were
alone. Gretel began
to cry.

"Do not cry," said
Hansel. "As soon
as the moon rises,
I will take you
home."

The moonlight shone
on the pebbles
Hansel had dropped
on the path.
They followed them
all the way home.

Some days later Hansel and Gretel heard their stepmother plotting again. When she was asleep, Hansel went to fill his pockets with pebbles.

The door was locked. He could not get into the garden. Gretel began to cry. "Do not cry," said Hansel. "I will think of something."

Next morning their
stepmother gave
them both a piece
of bread. Hansel
put his bread into
his pocket.
He broke it
into crumbs.

"Why do you always
look back?" asked
the woodcutter.
"I am watching
my pigeon," said
Hansel. But really
he was dropping
crumbs along
the path.

The children were left as before.
The moon rose. Hansel looked for
the crumbs. They were not there.
Birds had eaten them. Now Hansel
and Gretel were lost.
Three days passed. Then they saw
a white bird. "It wants us
to follow it," said Hansel.

Hansel and Gretel followed the bird.
It led them to a house with walls
made of gingerbread. It had
a roof made of cake and windows
made of sugar.

Hansel and Gretel were hungry. They
broke off a piece of the house.
They began to eat.
"Nibble nibble like a mouse.
Who is nibbling at my house?"
said a voice. The children thought
it was the wind and took no notice.

The door of the house opened.
An old woman came out.

The old woman asked them into the house. She gave them food to eat and a bed to sleep in.
The children thought she was kind. She was really a witch. She had made the gingerbread house to trap children. She ate children for dinner.

The witch shut Hansel in a stable.
It had bars in the door.
Then the witch woke Gretel.
"Cook something for your brother,"
she said. "I want to fatten him
up before I eat him."
Gretel wept, but she had to do as
she was told.

Hansel was given the best food.
Gretel was given the scraps. Every
day the witch made Hansel put his
finger through the bars. Every day
Hansel held out a bone instead of
his finger. The witch could not see
very well. Every day she said,
"Not fat enough yet!"

One day the witch could wait
no longer.
"Fetch some water, girl. Fill the
pot!" she said. When that was done,
she said, "Crawl into the oven, girl.
Make sure it is hot." The witch was
going to push Gretel into the oven.

Gretel guessed
what the witch was
going to do.
"I do not know how
to get into the
oven," she said.
"Silly girl!" said
the witch. "I will
show you."
Gretel stood
behind the witch.
She pushed the
witch into the oven.
She closed the door.

It only took a moment to free
Hansel. They filled their pockets
with treasure from the witch's house.
Then they set off to find their way
home. A white duck took them part
of the way.

At last they came to a part of
the forest they knew. Soon they saw
their own house.

The woodcutter was very glad to see
them. He told them their stepmother
was dead.

They sold the treasure and the three
of them lived happily ever after.

All these appear in the pages of
the story. Can you find them?

woodcutter

Hansel

Gretel

pebbles

bread

bird

witch

gingerbread house

Use the pictures to tell the story in your own words, and then draw your own pictures.

Thumbelina

Once there was a woman who wanted
a child. She went to see a witch.
The witch gave her a barleycorn.
It was a very special barleycorn.

The woman took
the barleycorn
home and planted
it. It grew into
a flower like
a tulip. The
petals were
tightly closed.

The woman kissed
the petals. They
opened. Inside
the flower was
a tiny girl no
bigger than the
woman's thumb. The
woman called the
child Thumbelina.

Thumbelina slept
in a cradle made
from a walnut
shell. The covers
were made from
flower petals.

Thumbelina played
in a boat made
from a tulip
petal.

One day an ugly toad hopped
through the window. The toad
wanted Thumbelina as a wife for
her son. The toad carried the
cradle away. Thumbelina was asleep
inside it.

The toad put the cradle on a lily leaf. She went to get a room ready under the mud.

When Thumbelina awoke she was afraid. Soon the toad came back. She took the cradle to the room. She left Thumbelina sitting on the lily leaf.

The fish did not
like to see
Thumbelina cry.
They nibbled
through the lily
stem. The leaf
floated down the
river. Thumbelina
went with it.

A butterfly pulled
the leaf some of
the way.

A big beetle
picked Thumbelina
up. It took her
to a tree.

The other beetles
thought Thumbelina
was ugly.
"Let her go," they
said.
The beetle put
Thumbelina down on
a daisy.

Thumbelina stayed
in the wood. She
lived by herself.
But she was never
lonely. The birds
were her friends.
Her clothes were
tattered and torn,
but she was never
cold. She was happy
all day long.

Then winter came.
The wind was very
cold. Thumbelina
tried to keep warm.

Snow began to fall.
Thumbelina wrapped
herself in a leaf.
If she did not
find somewhere
warm to stay she
would die.

Thumbelina went
into a field where
the corn had been
cut. She knocked
at a door. A field
mouse opened it
and asked her in.
"You can stay with
me as long as you
like," said the
field mouse.

The mole came on
a visit. He said
he would like to
marry Thumbelina.

Thumbelina and the field mouse
went to see the mole's house.
The mole led them along a dark
tunnel. On the way they passed
a swallow. It was lying very still.
"It's dead!" said the mole.
He pushed the swallow with his foot.

Thumbelina could not forget the swallow. She waited until the others were asleep. Then she went back to the tunnel.

She lay her head on the swallow's chest. Its heart was beating.
It was not dead. It had fainted because it was so cold. Thumbelina covered it up to make it as warm as she could.

Thumbelina went back to the
swallow the next night. It had
opened its eyes. Thumbelina looked
after the swallow all winter long.
It grew well and strong.

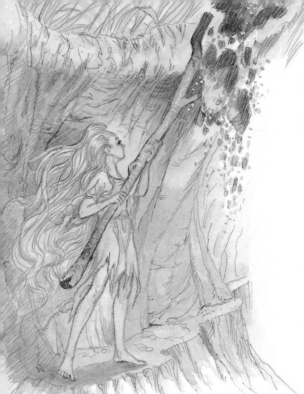

Spring came.
Thumbelina made
a hole in the roof
of the tunnel.
Now the swallow
could fly away.

"Sit on my back
and I will take
you with me," said
the swallow.
"I cannot," said
Thumbelina. "I am
to marry the mole."
She watched sadly
as the swallow
flew away.

The wedding day drew near.
Thumbelina sat all day at the
spinning wheel, spinning thread for
her wedding dress. Thumbelina was
unhappy. She did not like the mole.
She did not want to marry him. She
did not want to live underground
for the rest of her life.

It was Thumbelina's
wedding day. The
mole said she
could take one
last look at the
sun. Thumbelina
looked up at the
sky for the last
time. She heard
someone call.
It was the swallow.
"Come, fly with
me!" said the
swallow. This time
Thumbelina did.

The swallow took
Thumbelina to the
place where the
swallows make
their nests.

Near the nests were some white
flowers. Living inside the flowers
were tiny people like herself.

Thumbelina married the King of the tiny people. She wore a golden crown. She was given a pair of wings as a wedding present. Thumbelina changed her name to Maia and lived happily ever after.

All these appear in the pages of the story. Can you find them?

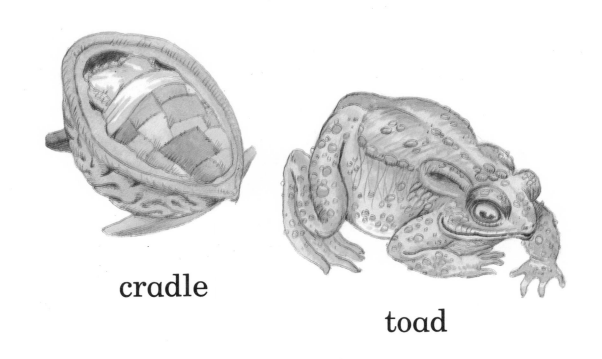

cradle

toad

fish

butterfly

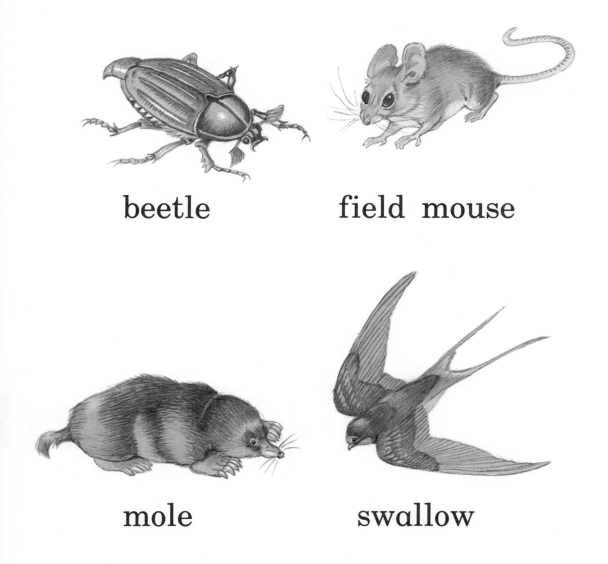

beetle   field mouse

mole   swallow

Use the pictures to tell the story
in your own words, and then draw
your own pictures.

The Little Mermaid

The King of the Sea and his family live in a palace on the seabed. Fish swim in and out of the palace all the time. The King's family have tails like the fish.

The King's daughters
are the mermaids.
They find things
from shipwrecks.
They put them
in their gardens.
One little mermaid
has a statue of
a boy in her
garden.

Her grandmother
tells her stories.
The little mermaid
likes stories
about people.

When mermaids grow up they can go
to the surface of the sea. This is
the first time the little mermaid
has been to the surface. The sea
is shiny and flat, like glass.
She can see a ship.

There is a prince
on the ship. He is
like the statue
of the boy in
her garden.

The wind begins to blow. There is
a storm coming. It starts to rain.
The ship is tossed by the waves.
Suddenly the ship turns over. It
is sinking. The prince is thrown
into the water. He is drowning.

The little mermaid does not want the prince to drown. She puts her arms round him. She stops him sinking. The waves take them to the shore. The little mermaid lays the prince on the sand. His eyes are closed but he is alive.

There is someone
coming. The little
mermaid hides
behind a rock. She
sees some girls.
The girls see the prince. They do
not see the little mermaid. They
carry the prince away.

The little mermaid
goes home to the
palace under the
sea. She sits in
her garden and
looks at the
statue of the boy.
She thinks about
the prince all
the time.

Her mermaid sisters find out where
the prince is living. They take the
little mermaid to the place.

The little mermaid
visits the bay
every night. She
watches the prince.
She cannot go
to him because
she cannot walk.
She has no feet.
Every night she is
more sad. "I will
ask the witch to
change my tail
into legs and
feet," she says.
"Then perhaps
the prince will
love me."

"I will help if you give me your voice," says the witch. The little mermaid loves to sing but she loves the prince more. "You will die if the prince ever loves another better than you!" warns the witch.

"Please do as
I ask," says the
little mermaid.
The witch mixes
her a potion.

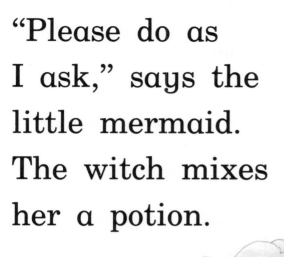

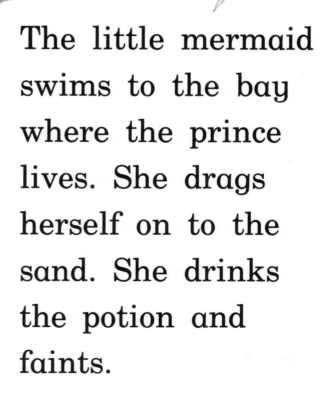

The little mermaid
swims to the bay
where the prince
lives. She drags
herself on to the
sand. She drinks
the potion and
faints.

When the little
mermaid opens her
eyes, the prince
is standing beside
her. "Who are
you?" he asks.
"Where have you
come from?"
She cannot answer
because she has
no voice.
The prince takes
her to his palace.
Her new feet hurt
with every step
she takes.

The little mermaid
dances gracefully.
Nobody knows how
much her new feet
hurt.

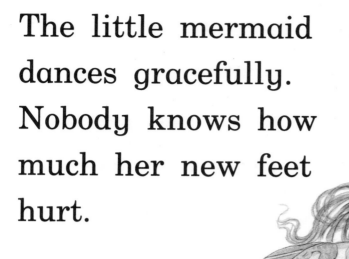

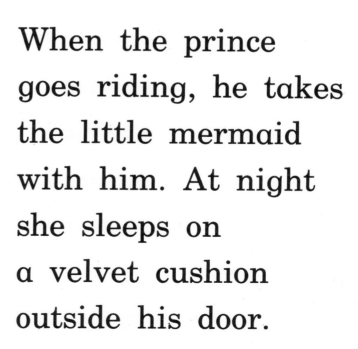

When the prince
goes riding, he takes
the little mermaid
with him. At night
she sleeps on
a velvet cushion
outside his door.

One night, when everyone is asleep, she goes to bathe her feet in the sea. Her sisters come to see her. They tell her they miss her. Her father and her grandmother are missing her too. They wave to her from some way off.

The prince grows to love the little mermaid like a sister. She is very happy. Then, one day, the King sends the prince to see a princess. The prince does not want to go. The King says he must.

As soon as the prince sees the
princess he wants to marry her.
The little mermaid remembers what
the witch said. She is very sad.
She knows she will die. On the day
of the wedding everyone is happy,
except for the little mermaid.

After the wedding they go on board
a ship. The little mermaid's sisters
follow the ship. They have cut off
their long hair. "We have found
a way to save you," they call
to the little mermaid. "We have
given the witch our hair. In return
she has given us a knife which
will break the spell."

Then the sisters shout to the little mermaid, "You must kill the prince. His blood must fall on your feet. Then your feet will turn back into a tail. You will be a mermaid again and you can come back to our palace under the sea."

The little mermaid looks at the sleeping prince. She cannot harm him. She would rather die herself. The little mermaid throws the knife into the sea. Then she throws herself into the sea. She changes into sparkling foam and is never seen again.

All these appear in the pages of the story. Can you find them?

King of the Sea   mermaid

statue   ship

prince

witch

knife

foam

Use the pictures to tell the story
in your own words, and then draw
your own pictures.